Anne Rockwell

Bumblebee, Bumblebee, Do You Know Me?

A GARDEN GUESSING GAME

HarperCollins*Publishers*

Bumblebee, bumblebee,
do you know me?
Yellow and green, I wave to the breeze
to say that spring is here.

I AM A DAFFODIL.

Butterfly, butterfly,
do you know me?
Here I stand, tall and straight,
while my silky cup catches rain.

I AM A TULIP.

June bug, june bug,
do you know me?
My leaves point like swords,
and my petals wave like flags.

I AM AN IRIS.

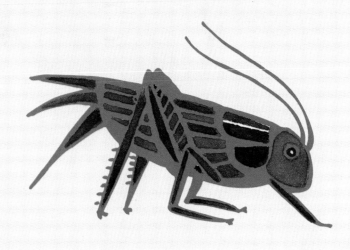

Cricket, cricket,
do you know me?
Watch me pop open!
See my tiny black seeds!

I AM A POPPY.

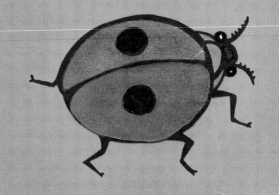

Ladybug, ladybug,
do you know me?
My thorns are prickly,
but my blossoms are soft.

I AM A ROSE.

Spider, spider,
do you know us?

We come in many colors,
and we turn our faces
to the summer sun.

WE ARE ZINNIAS.

Leafhopper, leafhopper,
do you know me?
You'll find me at breakfast
when my blue trumpet greets the day.

I AM A MORNING GLORY.

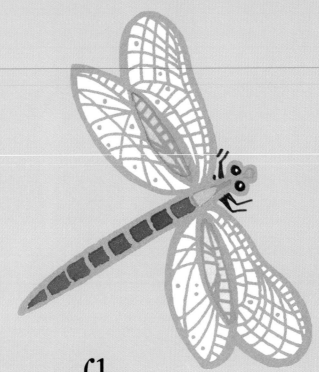

Dragonfly, dragonfly,
do you know me?
I'm curly and speckled.
My smell is the sweetest of all.

I AM A LILY.

Katydid, katydid,
do you know me?
Try and count my petals—
if you can!

I AM A DAISY.

Little boy, little boy,
do you know me?
My fuzzy stem
grows taller than you.
I am big and round
and golden.

Of course
I know you,
sunflower!
I know
all the flowers
I see.

For Phoebe and Sam

For the illustrations in this book, the author created
silk screens and painted them with watercolor and gouache.

Bumblebee, Bumblebee, Do You Know Me?
A Garden Guessing Game
Copyright © 1999 by Anne Rockwell
Printed in the U.S.A. All rights reserved.
http://www.harperchildrens.com

Rockwell, Anne F.
Bumblebee, bumblebee, do you know me? : a garden guessing game / by Anne
Rockwell.
    p.   cm.
  Summary: A series of riddles that first give descriptions of various flowers and then
reveal their names.
  ISBN 0-06-027330-5. — ISBN 0-06-028212-6 (lib. bdg.)
  [1. Flowers—Fiction.]   I. Title.
PZ7.R5943Bn 1999   97-28795
[E]—DC21   CIP
                                               AC

Typography by Christine Casarsa and Elynn Cohen
1 2 3 4 5 6 7 8 9 10
❖
First Edition